123 SESAME STREET®

Even Grouches Wear Masks!

By Andrea Posner-Sanchez
Story concept and design by Diane Choi

A Random House PICTUREBACK® Book

Random House 🏠 New York

© 2020 Sesame Workshop®, Sesame Street®, and associated characters, trademarks, and design elements are owned and licensed by Sesame Workshop. All rights reserved. Published in the United States by Random House Children's Books, a division of Penguin Random House LLC, 1745 Broadway, New York, NY 10019, and in Canada by Penguin Random House Canada Limited, Toronto, in conjunction with Sesame Workshop. Random House and the colophon are registered trademarks of Penguin Random House LLC.
rhcbooks.com
www.sesamestreet.org
Educators and librarians, for a variety of teaching tools, visit us at RHTeachersLibrarians.com
ISBN 978-0-593-42556-5 (trade) — ISBN 978-0-593-42557-2 (ebook)
Printed in the United States of America
10 9 8 7 6 5 4 3 2 1

Do you know why Elmo is wearing a mask? A mask keeps germs away so he stays healthy. By wearing a mask, Elmo helps to keep his friends and family healthy, too.

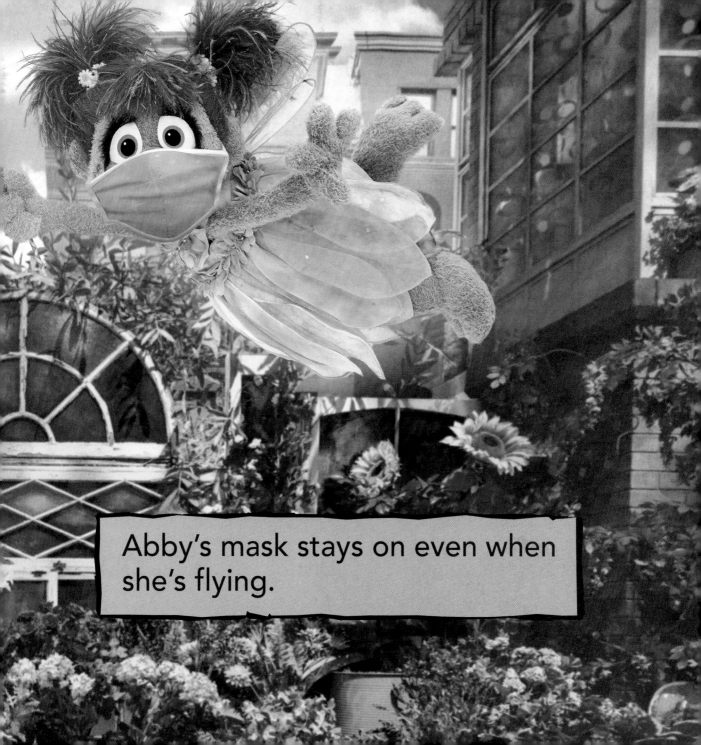

Abby's mask stays on even when she's flying.

Now all of Elmo's friends are wearing their masks and staying healthy.